Triple Trouble for Hound Dog Zip

Triple Trouble
for Hound Dog Zip

BY WILLIAM O. STEELE

ILLUSTRATED BY MIMI KORACH

GARRARD PUBLISHING COMPANY
CHAMPAIGN, ILLINOIS

G429418

Zip and the Fishing Contest

It was spring in the hill country of Tennessee. Fields were being plowed, corn planted, and new gardens forked up. Only one feller had time to sit on the front porch and whittle. His name was Tom.

Folks called him Foolish Tom, for he had been hiding behind a door when brains were handed out and so missed getting his share. Being simpleminded didn't bother Tom, for he had a dandy hound dog to take care of him.

Zip was the hound's name, and no one worked harder than he. His corn was planted before anybody else's, and he put up a fierce scarecrow to guard the field. His cabin was always neat as a new pin. His farm tools were kept sharp, and his smokehouse was always filled with meat. Zip and Foolish Tom got along just fine.

One morning Zip got out his axe. He was going to chop down trees to clear a new field for the farm. He had to work alone, for Foolish Tom was much too careless to use an axe.

Zip sharpened the axe on the grindstone. Then he said good-bye to Tom and left.

Foolish Tom went out front and sat down on the steps to play mumbly-peg. He couldn't handle an axe. He knew that. Zip said so. But Tom sure knew how to handle his single-blade knife. He was the best mumbly-peg player in the Tennessee hills.

Tom went through the many throws of the game. He flipped the knife from his elbows, knees, and head. Each time the knife landed with the blade in the ground. Now there was one last throw to make.

Foolish Tom was so busy playing mumbly-peg, he didn't see his neighbor Reuben Hill, who stopped at the rail fence to watch. Reuben had more money than the devil had sinners. But he was greedy and forever trying to get a heap more. He was scheming and shifty, and a body had to be mighty careful around him.

Tom took the knife blade between the thumb and the first finger of his right hand. With a backward snap of the wrist he flung it over his shoulder. He looked around and shouted with delight. The knife had landed upright, and Tom had gone through all the mumbly-peg throws without missing a one.

"That wasn't anything to shout about," snorted Reuben. "Any young 'un with a single-blade knife could do that."

Tom jumped in surprise. He thought he was all alone. But there stood Reuben Hill, big as life. "Morning, Reuben," said Tom. "A dandy day, ain't it?"

Reuben grunted. "It may look dandy to you," he answered, "but not to me. My old sow has run off. My corns hurt terrible bad, and I can't find a good cane to make me a new fishing pole for the contest."

Tom perked up, for he liked contests of all kinds.

Then Reuben told Tom about the fishing contest the next day. Tom would have to pay a dollar to enter, but he would get to keep all the fish he caught. Whoever caught the biggest fish would win the prize—a keg of Sheriff Brown's hand-squeezed apple cider.

Now there was nothing that made Foolish Tom smack his lips more than the thought of tasting the sheriff's cider. In all his born days he'd never had more than a drop or two of it. The sheriff held on to his cider like Reuben Hill held on to his money. He drank most of it himself and gave other folks just enough to let them know what they were missing.

"You come by for me in the morning, Reuben," Tom said, "and we'll go to Sheriff Brown's together."

"Fine," nodded Reuben. "Be ready early."

Tom promised he would, and they parted. Foolish Tom sat down right then and there in the middle of the road to figure out what kind of bait to use. Sheriff Brown hardly ever let folks

fish in his river. Tom reckoned there were whop-
pers just waiting to be caught if the right kind
of bait was used.

Foolish Tom had never won any contests for
thinking. Thoughts moved around in his head
as slow as sticky molasses. He sat there in the
roadway all morning pondering. Folks in buggies
and farmers in wagons drove around him. An
old sow with a litter of tiny piglets whuffled and
grunted at his bare toes. Nothing disturbed Tom.

9

Before Zip had left the house that morning, he had asked Tom to fix their dinner. When Zip arrived at noontime, tired and hungry, he found no sassafras tea, no fried side meat. There was no corn bread waiting for him. He didn't find Tom either, though he searched all through the cabin. He went out on the porch to call. Then he saw Foolish Tom sitting in the road, thinking as hard as ever.

"Whatever are you doing here?" he asked.

"Thinking," replied Tom.

Then he told Zip all about the contest Sheriff Brown was having tomorrow. Zip agreed that a dollar wasn't too much to pay for a contest, some fish, and a keg of the sheriff's cider.

"What are you aiming to use for bait?" Zip asked.

"I've been sitting in the road all morning thinking about that very thing," replied Tom. "And, Zip, I can't come up with one dern thing to use."

"How about digging up some red wiggly worms?" suggested Zip.

Foolish Tom slapped his leg and jumped

straight up in the air. "Now, why didn't *I* think of that?" he exclaimed. "Worms will be the very thing for bait."

Zip fixed their dinner and went back to work. Tom idled away the afternoon thinking about the contest.

The next morning it was still dark when Reuben reached Tom's house. "Foolish Tom! Come on!" he shouted.

Tom was ready with his cane fishing pole and his handful of worms. He said good-bye to Zip and set out along the road with Reuben. He marched along with his arm straight out before him and his fist closed tight.

"What's in your hand?" Reuben wanted to know.

Tom opened it and showed him. Reuben snorted, "Worms! Plain old worms. You won't catch a thing with them. Sheriff Brown's fish are plenty smart. You'll need better bait than worms."

Tom asked Reuben what he was going to use for bait.

"It's a mixture of tasty things that fish like,"

Reuben answered. "And *worms* ain't one of them."

"Do tell," said Tom.

By sunrise they reached the gate of Sheriff Brown's farm. There stood the sheriff, big and friendly.

"Drop your silver dollars in that there bucket," he said. They did. "Now you have officially entered my fishing contest. Don't forget—the winning fish has got to be caught in the river running through my farm. Mind now, it's to be

hooked by noontime to get that jug of apple cider."

Tom and Reuben nodded that they understood the rules. The sheriff wished them luck and sent them on their way across the fields. When they reached the river, folks were everywhere, fishing from logs and sandbars. Reuben complained they were so noisy the fish would all be scared away. He walked downstream to fish.

Foolish Tom liked folks and hollered greetings to each and every one. He headed upstream. At last he came to a big flat rock which stuck out over the river. Below, the water was still and as green as a bullfrog's back. It was just the spot he was looking for.

Tom went to the edge of the rock and peered over. "Hi, down there, fish," he called out cheerfully. "I've brought you a heap of tasty worms."

He slid a fat worm onto his hook and threw the line into the stream. He sat down with his legs dangling over the rock and the pole clutched in his hands.

As the morning passed, the day grew hot and

Tom got terribly sleepy. At last Tom decided to have a short nap.

He took the line from the pole and tied it around his right foot. Then he wound yards and yards of the fishing line around his ankle. If any fish so much as touched the bait, he was sure to feel it and wake up. He lay back and was soon snoring.

Now it happened that Reuben Hill had baited and rebaited his hook all morning long. He had fished up and down the river with his special tasty mixture. Still nothing, not even a mud turtle, nibbled at his bait.

As the sun climbed higher and higher, he worried more and more. The contest would soon end. Suppose Foolish Tom had caught a heap of fish with his stupid red worms. Then Tom and Zip would laugh at him. Reuben hated to have folks make fun of him.

He hid his pole and bait in the weeds and sneaked along the riverbank. He was feeling mean and ornery and ready to trick Foolish Tom. He made his way upstream until he found Tom asleep. Tom's legs were dangling over the rock,

and one leg had the line tied to it. That was the silliest way to fish that Reuben had ever seen.

Suddenly in the water below the rock there was a great commotion. A fierce whiskery face appeared at the surface and then sank. Tom's line went tight, and his leg jerked hard. He screamed as he was pulled off the rock into the river. Reuben roared with laughter. Tom splashed and spluttered, and Reuben laughed louder and louder.

At last Foolish Tom managed a watery yell. "Help! Oh, help, help, help, help!"

15

Reuben's eyes were streaming with tears of laughter.

"Help!" Tom cried again. "A big old fish is drowning me!"

At Tom's words Reuben stopped laughing. A wicked smile crossed his face. He dashed from the bushes and snatched up Tom's fishing pole and extended it toward Tom.

"Grab the cane," he called. "Grab the cane and I'll pull you out."

Tom had disappeared in the water. Bubbles came trailing up, and the water muddied and swirled. Reuben reckoned he might never see Foolish Tom and that fish again.

But at last Tom came up and grabbed the cane pole. Reuben pulled him to the bank. The big fish came along with him. It was a catfish. Reuben hauled Tom up the muddy bank and onto the grass. The fish came flopping along too.

Just at that moment Sheriff Brown and a crowd of folks arrived. "Who's yelling for help?" asked the sheriff. "What's going on here?"

Reuben explained the whole story, for Tom was too full of water and black river mud to talk. "And I won the prize," ended Reuben, "for I caught this here big fish."

"It . . . was . . . on my line," Tom spluttered.

"Yes," said Reuben, "but I was the one who pulled it out of the river to the bank. The one who pulls the fish in is the one who catches it. Isn't that right, sheriff?"

Sheriff Brown scratched his head. "I reckon it is," he said at last. "It sounds right, anyhow."

Tom had to admit that Reuben had pulled in the fish. The sheriff put the fish on the scales, and it weighed 39 pounds. He declared right then and there that Reuben Hill had caught the biggest fish of the morning and had won the apple cider.

That afternoon Reuben hitched his team of horses to the wagon. He went to fetch the fish and the cider. On the way back he found Tom and Zip and neighbor Huckley Botts waiting for him beside the road.

"Pleased to see you all," Reuben called out cheerfully. "I reckon you're waiting to get a squint at this huge catfish I caught."

18

"We are," said Zip. "We most certainly are."

"Oh, yes, indeedy," added Tom.

"Oh, my goodness, it is so," went on Huckley. They all three climbed into the wagon and looked at the big catfish. It stretched from one end of the wagon to the other. Its whiskers went from here to there. It was quite a sight.

"I see you ain't skinned and cleaned it yet," said Huckley.

"Naw," replied Reuben. "I wanted all the folks to see it just like it was when I caught it."

"There's nobody interested in this old fish but us three, Reuben," Huckley informed him. "We aim to cut it open and find my grandpa's special secret fishing lure."

"You're addled in the head, Huckley," Reuben said. "I saw the red worms Tom carried for bait."

"Those worms were just for show," Huckley told him. "Tom had the lure hid in his pocket all along. I told him not to tell you he was using it."

Reuben thought a moment. "What was the secret lure?" he asked at last.

"I oughtn't to tell you, Reuben. My old dead grandpa would be mad if he knew I told you," said Huckley. "But seeing as how you're sure to see it when we find it, I'll tell you—the lure is a shiny gold coin with turkey feathers tied to it."

"Do tell," whistled Reuben. "Wasting a gold coin for catching fish! Mercy, how foolish!" But his eyes lit up. "Your grandpa caught heaps of fish with this lure?"

"Oh, he did. He did," replied Huckley. "That's the reason I hate like sin to lose it. You sit still there. It won't take a minute for us to get the lure out."

Reuben nodded. Zip had a knife ready, and he slit that big old catfish from its nose to its tail.

Huckley got out his knife. "Sometimes it buries itself in a fish's liver," he said. "I'll just see." He cut off a piece of the fish.

"Hey!" cried Reuben. "That ain't the liver!"

Huckley was surprised. "I reckon it ain't," he replied and tossed the piece into the bushes.

"Now wait a minute," protested Reuben.

Tom now had his knife out and was cutting off big chunks of the fish. "Here it is," he sang out. "No, it ain't." He tossed that piece away and began to cut deeper into the catfish.

' "Hold on there!" bawled Reuben.

"Reuben," said Huckley, "don't you want us to find my lure? Do you want me to tell the sheriff you're hiding my secret family fishing lure?"

Reuben shook his head. He wanted to take the fish home and eat it all by himself.

The three searchers kept on cutting. Every now and then one of them would say, "My, this

is hot thirsty work." He'd pick up Reuben's cider jug and crook it over his arm and swig the contents deeply.

"Stop that!" screamed Reuben. He could hardly believe what was happening. His cider was disappearing. So was the fish.

But Zip and Tom and Huckley kept right on looking, hard as they could. The knives slashed and hacked, and in no time the big catfish was just a limp rag of skin and some bones.

Tom finished the last of the cider and threw down the jug. Zip stood up and wiped his knife on a whisp of straw.

"Whoooeee," said Huckley. "I do believe that lure must of got out by itself."

Tom scratched his head. "Come to think of it, maybe I never used that old lure," he said.

"We'd better go home right now and look," cried Zip. "That lure shouldn't be left lying around just any old where."

They jumped from the wagon and set off in a great hurry for Tom and Zip's cabin. Reuben stood in the dusty road. He looked at the ribbons that had been made of the big catfish and at the spoonful of cider left in the bottom of the jug. He looked and looked. Then he opened his mouth and began to bawl curses at the three. The horses took fright and kicked up their heels. They ran off with the wagon bouncing along.

Reuben sighed, moaned, pulled his hair, and shook his fists. At last he quieted down and walked off toward his farm.

Zip and Tom and Huckley Botts trotted to Tom's house. And my goodness—there was no sign of Huckley's grandpa's lure anywhere in the cabin!

Huckley hadn't entered the fishing contest, for that morning he had gone over into the next county to fish with his kinfolks. He had come back with a great mess of fish. Now they were all cleaned and ready for cooking. Zip, Tom, and Huckley were hungry after that day's work. So Zip heated up the skillet, and in a shake of a lamb's tail those fish were fried up crisp and brown and hot. Alongside them was a great heaping pile of cornmeal hoecakes.

The three began to eat, and soon the platters of food were empty. Tom wiped his greasy mouth

on the back of his hand and settled back into his chair. "My, those fish were good," he said.

"These fish were a sight better than that big catfish would have tasted," said Zip. "Likely it was old and tough."

"I reckon you're right," added Huckley. "And my stars, didn't we have fun outfoxing Reuben?"

They all leaned back in their chairs and laughed fit to bust.

"I declare," Zip said, "I do believe we got our dollar's worth from Sheriff Brown's fishing contest!"

Zip and the Talking Shoes

The hickory leaves were turning yellow, and the maple leaves were turning red and orange. Persimmons waited for the first frost to ripen. Days grew shorter, and chickens went to roost earlier. It was fall, and there was much work to do on the farm.

One day Zip said to Tom, "We've got to dig a stock pond up here next to the barn. That old one leaks and is dry most every winter. The cow don't like walking way down to the creek for a drink of water."

26

Zip took a string and tied it around the open end of a sack of corn. "Why don't you begin the pond while I take this corn to the mill to grind?" he asked Tom.

Tom rocked back and forth in his rocking chair. "Well," he said at last, "I can't dig now. I got something else to do today."

Zip said that was all right. He swung the bag to his shoulder and set out for the mill.

Tom watched till Zip was out of sight. Then he ran and got out a clean handkerchief. He put it in his pocket and skedaddled out to the road.

He stood there for a long time. Now what Tom wanted was to get a job of work and earn some money. The truth was he was so foolish he didn't know how to go about it. So he just stood by the road waiting for something to happen. Nothing did.

Next morning Zip said, "It's a nice clear day. We'd better start digging that stock pond." But Tom replied, "Can't. Got something else to do today."

Once again Zip said it was all right. He went

out to the smokehouse and took down a ham. He was fixing to trade the meat for some red-top clover seed. Off he went with the ham.

Tom walked down to the side of the road and waited for his job of work. But a job offer didn't come along.

Now, Tom was interested in earning some money for a very special reason. He wanted a pair of pretty high-top shiny shoes like Reuben Hill's—shoes that *would talk to him.* Reuben's shoes talked every step he took. They said, "Squeaky-creaky-croaky-creaky-squeak!"

Tom could hardly believe his ears when he first heard Reuben's shoes talk. He thought it would be a fine thing to walk around in beautiful shiny shoes and listen to them say, "Squeaky-creaky-croaky-creaky-squeak!" And they would be such company when he was alone.

Oh, he wanted them so bad. He wanted to earn the money all by himself and surprise Zip. But Tom just didn't know how. So at last he lay down in the dust in the road and began to cry and moan.

Now who should come down the road just

then but mean old Reuben Hill. He had on his beautiful shoes.

Reuben cried out, "What ails you, Tom? Have you got the collywobbles or the limberneck? Or the itching quizzles?"

Tom couldn't take his eyes off Reuben's beautiful shoes. He just lay there in the dust looking at them and wanting them so bad.

"No," he told Reuben. "It ain't nothing like that."

"It ain't?" asked Reuben. "What is it then?" As Reuben moved, the shoes said, "Squeaky-creaky-croaky-creaky-squeak!"

"What it is," explained Tom, "is that I want me a job of work and I don't know how to get one."

"Why, is that all?" cried Reuben. "I can fix that nice as pie. Widow Tate has been looking for a feller to cut her corn and shock it. Run on down the road to Widow Tate's and get yourself a job of work."

Tom could scarcely believe his ears. Reuben was actually being nice to him. He said, "Thank you, kindly," and ran to Widow Tate's house.

She was mighty pleased to see Tom, and set him to work right away. Tom worked hard cutting the stalks of corn and standing them in shocks to dry.

When it was done, Tom went up to the widow's back door and knocked on it. She opened the door, and he asked for his pay.

"Pay?" said the widow. "Why, I gave the money to Reuben yesterday. He said he'd take care of everything."

So Tom hurried over to Reuben's farm. Reuben was sitting on his front porch trimming his toenails with the sheep shears. He had used Tom's wages to buy a fine new pair of shoes, and he didn't want his flint-hard toenails poking holes in the leather.

"Now, you give me my pay, Reuben Hill!" bawled Tom, running up on the porch.

"What pay is that?" asked Reuben.

"For the work I did at Widow Tate's," yelled Tom. "You took my money, Reuben. You know you took it!"

"Now, you just hold your horses," Reuben answered. "You asked me for a job of work, and I gave it to you, Tom. You never said a word about money."

Tom thought hard. At last he reckoned Reuben was right. Money hadn't been talked about at all. He'd gotten the job of work he wanted, and he'd done it right and proper.

Still, here he was without money or shoes. Somehow Reuben had tricked him once again.

"Whatever did you mean to do with the money, Foolish Tom?" Reuben asked.

"I aimed to buy me a pair of squeaky shoes just like you got!" Tom said sadly.

"You did!" cried Reuben. "Why didn't you say so? Since I got a new pair of shiny yellow pointed shoes, I'll let you have my ole squeaky ones."

Tom brightened at once.

"Clean out the cow stalls in the barn. Then the shoes will be yours to keep forever," Reuben told him.

Tom worked terribly hard the rest of the day at Reuben's. Darkness was coming on as he hurried home with his talking shoes in his hands.

After he had left, Reuben did a little dance of joy. He had a brand-new pair of shoes he had bought with Tom's wages. For his own two no-good shoes he had gotten a half day's work out of Tom. It was one of the happiest days of Reuben's life.

To make himself even more happy, he followed Tom home to see the fun. Zip was sure to have a conniption fit when Foolish Tom told him about the day's doings. Reuben didn't want to miss a bit of it.

Zip was standing at the kitchen window worrying about Tom. Finally he saw him hurrying along the road. He could see a shadowy figure following Tom, and he recognized Reuben Hill. Zip went and sat in the rocking chair and waited to hear what Tom had been up to.

Foolish Tom came busting through the door holding up his shoes. "Looky here, Zip, what I got—" cried Tom, "a pair of talking shoes!" He told Zip about working for Widow Tate and cleaning out the cow stalls in Reuben Hill's barn.

Zip took the shoes and inspected them. They were cracked on the sides. The soles were loose, and the heels were worn out. He handed them back to Tom without a word. Tom put them on and walked back and forth across the kitchen. The shoes went "Squeaky-creaky-croaky-creaky-squeak!"

"Oh, don't they talk good!" Tom exclaimed.

Zip gave a quick glance at the window to make sure Reuben was there. "I do declare," Zip said, "they do talk. Let me get a little closer and hear what they're saying."

So Zip leaned close to the floor with his paws behind his ears. Tom walked back and forth before him. The shoes squeaked loudly for Zip.

"I do believe those shoes of yours are saying something about treasure," Zip said in a loud voice. "Walk around one more time, Tom."

Tom moved slowly across the room.

"I can't make out everything your shoes are saying about the treasure," Zip said, standing up, "but 'the lower side of our barn' I heard

plain as can be. Tom, I believe this time you got the best of Reuben Hill. If he only knew that his shoes have told us about the buried treasure! Why, he'd have a running fit for letting his talking shoes get away from him."

"Let's go to digging right now!" cried Tom. "There's nothing I like better than digging up treasure."

"Not now, Tom," answered Zip. "Let's eat our supper first."

Zip saw Reuben's head disappear from the window. He set about fixing supper. Tom strutted about the kitchen proud as a turkey gobbler. The shoes squeaked and squeaked. Finally Zip had to take the shoes away and make Tom sit at the table and eat. Then he sent him to bed.

Zip covered the dishes of leftover food with a cloth. He blew out the candle and eased out the door onto the back porch. A dim yellow light glowed from the lower side of the barn. Every once in a while there was the sound of a spade striking rock.

"I declare, I believe that must be Reuben Hill digging for treasure down by our barn," Zip said to himself with a smile. "He's going to save me and Tom a heap of work. We were going to have to dig us a stock pond there. Now Reuben is kind enough to dig it for us."

He was grinning as he went to bed. The next morning, sure enough, there was a fine hole by the barn. When Zip came back from inspecting it, he told Tom he had to go buy a milk pail. He said that if Reuben Hill came by

wanting to buy the shoes, Tom was not to sell
them. "Don't tell him about the treasure," cau-
tioned Zip.

Tom promised he wouldn't. He put on his
shoes and went outside. It wasn't long before
Reuben came by and admired the shoes.

"I sure do miss those old talking shoes," Reuben
said. "They're a heap of company."

"Sure are," agreed Tom.

"Tell you what," said Reuben. "I'll swap you
my new shoes for my old ones."

"No sir-ree bobtail goat," Tom exclaimed with a shake of his head. "Zip said for me not to give them to you."

"Well, you don't have to do what Zip says all the time," smiled Reuben. "I'll just take off these new shiny shoes and set them on the porch. I'll put five silver dollars inside. You can have the new shoes and money for those old shoes." Reuben put the shoes on the porch and stood there barefooted.

Tom wouldn't trade, though the silver dollars tempted him. Reuben begged and begged, but Tom wouldn't listen. At last Reuben said, "I sure miss them old shoes. I've almost forgotten how they squeaked. Foolish Tom, don't be so cruel hearted. Let me hear them one more time."

Tom agreed to let him listen to his talking shoes. "But, Reuben," he said, "if they talk about treasure, you're to stop up your ears. Don't listen, or Zip will be mad."

"Oh, fiddle-faddle, Tom. You know I won't pay no attention to what the shoes say," replied Reuben. "I just want to hear that pretty music one more time." He dropped to his knees in the front yard. Then he put his head on the ground so he surely wouldn't miss a thing the shoes told him.

Tom walked past. The shoes said, "Squeaky-creaky-croaky-creaky-squeak!"

"That's mighty pretty," exclaimed Reuben. "Walk by me some more, Tom."

Foolish Tom pranced back and forth close to Reuben's ear. Now Reuben was trying so hard to hear what the shoes were saying, he didn't notice that Zip had come back. Zip was standing in the road watching Reuben. Reuben didn't notice that Huckley Botts, Widow Tate, and several other folks had also stopped to watch.

Finally Widow Tate spoke up. "Good gracious sakes, Reuben Hill, what are you doing?" she called out. Reuben jumped and looked around. He saw all those people staring at him. His mouth fell open, and he turned red as a calico handkerchief. But he didn't get up, and he didn't say anything.

"I reckon he has lost his mind," said Huckley Botts.

"You'd think from looking at him that he was

listening to Tom's shoes," said Zip. "That's sure a wild crazy thing to do."

"He's acting strange, for certain sure," nodded Huckley. "Maybe we'd better send for the sheriff."

Reuben got redder and redder. "Don't tell those folks what I was doing," he whispered to Tom. "You don't want all them folks to know about your talking shoes."

"I reckon you'd sure have to be crazy to listen to shoes," laughed Zip.

"Maybe we ought to lock him up in the hen house," Huckley said. "He might get violent. He might do somebody harm."

"Tom," whispered Reuben desperately, "if you won't tell what I was doing, I'll give you my new shoes and the silver dollars. You can keep the old ones too."

Tom didn't answer. He just went on listening to his shoes saying, "Squeaky-creaky-croaky-creaky-squeak!"

By and by Zip walked over and stood by Reuben, who was still down on his knees. Then he turned and said to the folks gathered in the road, "It's all right. Reuben ain't crazy. He's just looking at Tom's feet to make sure those new shoes he gave Tom will fit. Ain't that right, Reuben?"

Reuben scrambled up. "That's right," he said. "That's all I was doing." By this time he was very red. He looked like he was going to blow into a hundred and eleven pieces.

"My, they are just the right size," said Zip. He looked into the new yellow pointed shoes.

"I think they'll fit just right, especially with those fancy silver linings."

"Well, I reckon things are all right then," said Widow Tate. She and the others started on their way. Reuben dashed through the gate. He ran down the road toward his house as fast as he could.

Tom was so entranced with his shoes that he never even noticed Reuben was gone. "My goodness, Zip," cried Tom. "Just listen here to my shoes. Don't they sound lovely? Whatever are they saying now?"

Tom walked back and forth. Zip cocked his head to one side. He listened a moment and then said, "Well, Tom, those shoes are saying that Reuben Hill is mean and greedy, but you're merely foolish."

And they each picked up one of the new shoes with the silver dollars inside and went into the cabin.

Zip and the Terrible Snout

One fine morning Tom was sitting in the
rocking chair taking it easy. Zip hoped to join
him when he finished churning for butter. While
he was moving the dasher up and down, suddenly the bottom came out of the old churn.
Milk went sloshing all over the kitchen floor.
Zip had to clean up the mess. Then he sent
Tom to the trading store to fetch a new churn.

Foolish Tom set out at once. Without a single
mishap he got to the store and bought the churn.

Then, clutching it proudly in his arms, he headed back home.

Now there was another customer in the store. It was Reuben Hill. He was back behind the plows and horse collars, buying a long piece of black stovepipe. Tom didn't see Reuben, but Reuben saw Tom.

After Tom had left the store, Reuben picked up the stovepipe and went out too. He climbed up on his wagonload of hay and clucked to the horses. They began to amble down the same road Foolish Tom had taken. As Reuben rode along, his brains were bubbling with mischief all the while. The devil inside him was urging him to do something bad to Tom.

At last Reuben pulled off the road into the shade and set to work. He shifted the bales of hay around until he had a hiding place at the front of the wagon. He left small cracks between several of the bales so that he could see to drive, but no one could see him. Then he collected the horses' reins and hid himself behind the bales. He yelled at the horses, and the wagon started off down the road once again.

All this time Tom was marching along in grand style, and singing fit to bust:

Had a fine cow, she wouldn't give milk.
Whackedy whang doodledy-dooo.
Sat by the fire in a dress of silk.
Whackedy whang doodledy-dooo.
Sewed pretty seams with thimble and thread.
Whackedy whang doodledy-dooo.
Slept in the cabin in a four poster bed.
OHHHH, whackedy whang doodledy-dooo.

When he stopped to get his breath, he heard something coming down the road, and he turned around. Rolling toward him was a team of horses pulling a wagonload of hay. He didn't see the driver, but he began to wave at the wagon to get a ride the rest of the way home.

Nobody waved back, for the driver's seat was empty. The horses' reins disappeared right smack into the hay.

"Why gracious," Tom said, "I never knew hay had sense enough to drive a wagon."

The horses plodded steadily on as the reins

slapped against their backs. The wheels turned
merrily. The load of hay drove itself nearer and
nearer.

Then the hay spoke in a deep, scary voice.
"Howdy, there, Foolish Tom."

Tom was powerful uneasy. He'd never had a
load of hay speak to him before, but he guessed
it would be only polite to return the greeting.
"Howdy . . . oh, howdy, hay," he stammered. "I
mean . . . howdy, mister load of hay." But that
didn't sound right, so he tried again, "Hey . . .
howdy . . . hay."

The horses plodded on past Tom. As the wagon went by, a long, black, fierce-looking snout suddenly appeared from the hay. It moved toward Foolish Tom. He jumped up in the air and screamed like a wildcat. He threw the churn at the snout while he was still off the ground. Tom came down running and took off like chained blue lightning.

The churn missed the stovepipe snout, bounced off the hay, and fell under the wagon. The wheels rolled over it with a loud scrunching sound. The horses came to a halt, and Reuben

jumped out of his hiding place. He looked at the cedar churn. The metal bands were twisted; the wooden dasher and sides were splintered. He leaned against the hay and laughed and laughed.

"That churn is plumb dead," he gasped at last. "It ain't smart for churns to tangle with hay wagons."

He climbed back on the wagon and rode off, chuckling and guffawing at the thought of the black snout of stovepipe that almost ate Foolish Tom.

Now Tom was badly frightened. He knew
that horrible big snout would have swallowed
him whole. He ran and ran. He sprinted through
a thicket and out the other side with little trees
and vines hanging from him. On through a field
of corn he charged. Stalks and crows and grass-
hoppers flew every which way. He slammed right
into a chicken house and knocked it flat. Then
he raced on with hens riding on his shoulders
and squawking for dear life.

At last he reached a hog wallow and dived into it. The wallow was filled with big pigs and little pigs cooling in the mud. Foolish Tom lay down among the pigs with just his nose sticking out. There he stayed, shivering and shaking till it was dark. Suddenly the light from Zip's lantern shone out across the pig lot. "Tom!" called Zip. "Where are you?"

"I'm in the pig wallow," Tom called back. Only he forgot he was under the mud. So what he really said was, "Shubbly, blub, bubbly mub bub."

Zip heard him and helped him to get out. As he scraped the mud from poor Tom's face and hands and clothes, he said, "Foolish Tom! Why, I declare, what am I ever going to do with you?"

"There was this big wagonload of hay, and it spoke to me," Tom answered. His teeth still chattered. "It said howdy to me, plain as day, and I spoke back to it. But it must not have liked what I said. Just then a blood-sucking black snout came out of the hay and reached for me with slurping noises."

"I know about it," said Zip. "Slim Tolliver saw it all, and he told me about it."

"Did it go for Slim too?" asked Tom. "Did it try to suck out his liver and his heart and his eyeballs?"

"No, it didn't," replied Zip. "It was just a piece of black stovepipe Reuben Hill bought at the store."

"But it waved around and made fearsome slushing sounds," said Tom.

"Well, if it did, it was Reuben who was hiding among the bales of hay," Zip explained. "He's the cause of our churn being busted, but I reckon I'll never get him to admit it, much less pay for a new one."

Tom didn't say another word. He hung his head. Reuben had tricked him once more. Zip comforted Tom the best he could, and they went back to the house.

As the days went by, Reuben told everyone far and wide about the trick he had played on Foolish Tom. It made Tom feel mighty bad.

Zip was worried about more than Tom's feelings. Buying that new churn had taken all their savings. Now the money box was empty, and they didn't have a new churn. The milk clabbered, and Tom and Zip had to eat grease drippings on their bread.

One day Slim Tolliver passed the cabin. He saw Zip walking about the front yard mighty troubled. "My goodness, Zip, what ails you?" he called out.

Zip told him what the matter was—that he and Tom had no churn because of Reuben's meanness. They couldn't buy a new one, for they didn't have any money. Zip would have to find time to pick and sell lots of blackberries and huckleberries.

Slim scratched his head. "Seems like there should be some way to make Reuben pay for that churn," he said at last.

Zip paced about again for a while. Finally he said, "I reckon there is, Slim, if you'd help me just a little bit."

He and Slim began to confabulate.

Just beyond Reuben's farm the road forked. One fork led to town and the store. The other one went up Lick Skillet Hollow. Nobody had

lived up there for ages. Hardly anybody ever used that road.

Right after midday Zip went by Reuben's farm and up Lick Skillet Hollow. Halfway up the hollow was a wolf pit. Long ago some early settler had dug it to trap wolves. Nobody knew about it but Zip. On this afternoon he went up the hollow and looked at the pit. He'd always reckoned it might be useful someday. He cleaned it out pretty good. Then he laid some branches and leaves over the top, so no little animals would fall in.

The next day Reuben saw Slim Tolliver's wife and her oldest boy taking the road to Lick Skillet Hollow. "Howdy!" he yelled, but they didn't answer.

Soon a man from the other side of the county went by, taking the same road. Reuben watched. Then in a spell two more men walked by. After them came a woman wearing a poke bonnet. Not one of them returned Reuben's "Howdy!"

All this puzzled Reuben. "Where are you headed, neighbor?" he asked the next man to pass.

The man shook his head and hurried on without answering.

Then along came Slim Tolliver on his old gray mare, holding something in front of him. It was a thing-a-my-jigger of wire and wheels and springs. Reuben had never seen anything like it before, but he knew it must be something terribly important. It must have something to do with the goings-on up Lick Skillet Hollow. Maybe it was a gold finder!

"Slim!" shouted Reuben, "what in creation you got there?"

56

Slim Tolliver didn't answer. He didn't even look around. He just rode right on by Reuben with the contraption and took the fork leading up the hollow.

Reuben was about to split wide open with curiosity. He had to know what all the commotion was about. He knew he would find out if he followed Slim and watched what he did with that thing-a-my-jigger. So he tagged along behind Slim, sneaking along the roadside. He kept out of sight behind trees and bushes.

Slim rode along very slowly. At last he stopped, got off his horse, and tied it to a bush. Then he walked along the path through the woods holding the contraption in his hands. The thing of wire and springs and wheels made a strange clacking noise. Suddenly Slim began to walk fast, and Reuben ran to keep up.

Slim went around a bend in the path and stepped quickly into the bushes. He was hidden by the thick leaves.

Reuben rushed along the path, listening for the strange clacking noise. He couldn't hear a thing, so he ran harder. Just as he was rounding a bend, the ground suddenly gave way beneath him. With a yell Reuben fell into the wolf pit.

Now that pit was deep, and the sides were straight. Reuben was big and fat. Try as he might, he couldn't get out. He couldn't jump out, and he couldn't scramble up the sides either.

He began to holler, "Help! Help! It's me, Reuben Hill!"

Nothing happened. "Help! Oh, help!" bawled Reuben again. Soon a face looked over the edge. It was Slim Tolliver. Reuben still had his mouth open, bellowing. Slim jumped like he was scared almost to death.

"Oh, it's the devil himself," he cried. He skedaddled away down the path.

"Come back! Come back!" roared Reuben. But Slim just ran on.

Reuben sat down on the trash at the bottom of the pit. He didn't see how he was ever going to get out. He almost felt sorry for all the mean things he'd done in his life.

After a long time he heard somebody coming, and he began to holler once more. Suddenly Zip looked down at him. "I heard tell," he said, "that the devil was here, coming up out of the ground belching fire and brimstone."

"Zip, you know I ain't the devil," Reuben said.

"No, I reckon not," replied Zip. "At least you ain't got no horns on your head."

"I need help to get out of this pit," pleaded Reuben.

"I'll try to find a rope," Zip told him. He left quickly. It wasn't long before he was back,

saying he couldn't find a rope anywhere in the settlement.

Reuben put his head against the side of the pit and groaned. Then he looked up and said, "Zip, you get me out, and I'll give you that old buggy sitting in my barn."

"I got no use for an old buggy or a new one either," Zip replied.

Reuben ground his teeth in frustration. He hated to spend his money.

"Well, I tell you what, Zip," he sighed. "You get me out, and I'll buy a brand-new cedar churn for you and Tom."

"All right, Reuben," nodded Zip. "I'll try to find a ladder."

Zip returned after dark carrying a lantern. "Reuben," he called, "you still down there?"

"Where else could I be?" growled Reuben angrily. "Did you get a ladder?"

"Sure didn't, Reuben," Zip answered. "The folks are all using their ladders."

"Oh, Zip, I've got to get out," wailed Reuben. "I'll give you a churn, a stone jar to keep your butter in, and one of my little heifer calves."

"All right," replied Zip. "You sit tight right there."

Zip was gone and gone and gone. Daylight had come to Lick Skillet Hollow before Zip showed up at the pit again.

"Where in thunderation have you been?" screamed Reuben. "Don't you know I'm down here suffering?"

Sheriff Brown stuck his head over the edge and asked, "You all right, Reuben?"

"Of course I'm not!" bellowed Reuben. "Get me out of here!"

"Reuben, we ain't been able to find a ladder or a rope or anything," Zip told him. "Everybody's using those things. Ain't none to be had in the whole county."

Suddenly Reuben was scared. He was afraid he was going to have to stay in the wolf pit forever and ever and just waste away to nothing at all. He was scared through and through, and he was desperate. He was so desperate, he offered to buy the sheriff a brand-new cook stove for the jail. "And Zip," he went on, "I'll add several new pairs of overalls to all of those other

things I promised you and Tom. Just get me out quick!"

Zip turned to the sheriff. "We've got to help him," he said. "He's pretty bad off now, and he might get worse." Sheriff Brown agreed. "But, sheriff," added Zip in a loud voice so Reuben would be sure to hear, "me and you have gone to a heap of trouble to come and help Reuben. And our troubles ain't over yet. What if Reuben refuses to pay for the help we give him?"

"He'll go to jail for the rest of his life," the sheriff answered in a terribly loud official voice. "A man's promise is plumb legal in my county. It's binding, and it's exflunkquotious too."

"Exflunkquotious!" repeated Zip in awe. "That can be mighty bad on a feller I hear tell."

"Ohhhhh!" sobbed Reuben. "I'll keep my promise. I will! Just get me out! Out!" He covered his face with his hands and groaned terribly.

So Zip got some heavy pieces of grapevine and a long pole. He and the sheriff finally managed to get Reuben Hill out of the wolf pit and safely home.

Once home, Reuben took to his bed and stayed there for days bemoaning his ill luck.

At last he got his strength together and went to the store with a purse full of large clinking coins. He bought everything he had promised for Zip and Tom and Sheriff Brown. Spending so much money made him turn green and sickly, and he had to go back to bed for a long time to recover.

Later when Foolish Tom was trying on his stiff new overalls, he said, "Zip, here's a riddle I made up. What drives all by itself and has a long black snout sticking out of its middle?"

"I can't imagine," grinned Zip. "What on earth can it be?"

"A load of hay," replied Tom.

"Well, I declare, that's a fine riddle," nodded Zip.

Tom moved toward the door. "I'm going to the barn to show the new little calf my overalls," he said.

"You do that," Zip told him. "And Foolish Tom, please, please try to stay out of trouble down there."